Interludes From Melancholy Falls Volume 1

By

Jeff Heimbuch

Cover Design by Vivian Kulkowski

ISBN: 1982079096
ISBN-13: 978-1982079093

For Martina, who has been forced to live in Melancholy Falls just as long as I have. I love you, sweet pea.

CONTENTS

INTRODUCTION

Interludes are the stories of the people of Melancholy Falls.
Sometimes they involve the main characters. Often they don't.

These are some of those stories.

1
INDISPOSED

This speech was made publicly in front of City Hall earlier this week.

Hello. My name is Pamela DePalma, and I am the former Mayor of Melancholy Falls.

I am here before you today to announce my campaign to run for re-election as Mayor, after being unfairly ousted last year in a surprise election that I was in no way able to participate in. I was indisposed.

Yes, I realize I was indisposed for the better part of a year. However, while I was unable to make public appearances, I was still able to complete my job to the best of my ability and work to make Melancholy Falls the best town in New Jersey. I have loved and served this town for most of my adult life in some form of public service, and I would love nothing more to take back the role of Mayor that was taken from me.

While the reasoning behind my being indisposed has never been publicly discussed, I feel it is high time to reveal the truth, especially in light of the fact that our current Mayor is a vengeful wraith. If the people of Melancholy Falls can accept her station in life, and still elect her to office, then I feel like they would also sympathize with mine.

As you know, politics is a dirty game. Often, throughout a

politician's career, they will be called many hurtful names by opponents hoping to knock them down a peg or two. Most people realize that politicians are rats. I have accepted and expected to be referred to as that throughout my career, and gladly took it all in stride. It came with the territory.

However, I never expected to be a rat in the most literal sense.

Yes, during my fourteenth month in office, I was transformed into a rodent that most people find disgusting and a bane to our town. Though I was stuck in this form for almost a year, while still fulfilling my duties as Mayor. While this change was most definitely not by choice, I still was steadfast in my dedication to my work, and was still unceremoniously removed from office.

Yes, I know, there are probably many questions. Allow me to explain what transpired to invoke this change in me.

As most of you know, the public restrooms at Werner Park have been an issue of debate for many years. While mostly deemed clean enough for human use, a small group of citizens were concerned about the rat population that was growing nearby. These rats have inhabited our town for many years, and have been considered docile by local animal control. However, these citizens were concerned that said creatures were getting too close for comfort to the restrooms, and were afraid to use them.

While I initially agreed with them on this, I created a task force to peacefully trap and re-locate these critters. However, a few days into this, I received a phone call from a member of said task force, asking me to meet with them at the Werner Park restrooms. As a public servant, I thought nothing of receiving this request at 2:37AM in the morning, and went immediately.

Upon arrival, I was ambushed; not by the task force, but by the rats themselves. While the exact circumstances of the 'how' it occurred are still unclear to me, the next thing I remember, I was no longer towering over them. Instead, I was more on their level, literally. I was a rat myself.

Initially, I freaked out. Of course, who wouldn't? But in time, I came to learn that the leader of the rat colony, Nigel Ratigan, was the one who ordered the change in me. Using their rat magic, they brought me into their world to help me understand what exactly was going on, their issues and troubles, and why they were getting closer to the Werner Park restrooms.

This was all done using their own language, Ratenese, which, somehow during the change, I was now able to understand.

According to Nigel, the rats of Melancholy Falls had lived peacefully and co-existed with all creatures, big and small. However, over the years, a rivalry has been taken up between them and the population of were-bunnies. Though Nigel and his colony tried to remain peaceful at first, the were-bunnies became more and more aggressive. Being the simple and non-violent colony that they were, rather than stay and fight, the rats migrated elsewhere. However, the were-bunnies followed. They were relentless, and seemed to have a vendetta against them.

The latest place for the rats to have settled were the restrooms at Werner Park. It was here that they finally felt safe again. They wished no harm upon their human neighbors using the restrooms...they merely needed a place to live. They turned me into a rat to help me understand that, and to show me how we could live together in harmony.

Once Nigel fully explained the situation, he set forth to return me to my human form. However, due to an issue with their magic, they were unable to do so. And so, I was trapped as a rat until further notice.

I returned to my office at City Hall to discuss the matter with my team. Though I was no longer able to speak English, only Ratenese, I soon created a language with my staff using a typewriter and a complicated series of squeaks in order to communicate.

This is how I continued to fulfill my duties as Mayor while in that form. I was indisposed, but only in the sense that I was unable to make public appearances. It wasn't the most perfect of situations, but my entire team made the best of it. We still did a damn good job. In fact, I accomplished MORE as a rat than any other human based life form has ever done while in the office of Mayor.

Which brings us to today. Very recently, despite some complications in the process, I was able to mostly return to my human form. Please do not mind my tail.

I have learned much during my time as a rat, such as a better understanding of our town, and appreciation for all things, big or small. I have also learned how to love, as my new husband, Nigel, can attest. But I stand before you today to tell you that there is no better candidate for Mayor of Melancholy Falls than I.

I, who have seen this town from a new angle, in a new light. I, who have served you well in the past and want to serve you even better in the future. I, who will run on a strict anti-were-bunny campaign, to help end a menace that has long plagued Melancholy Falls from the shadows.

The road back to the Mayor's office may be hard, but by golly, I will fight for it.

Citizens, hear me! My name is Pamela DePalma, and I am no longer indisposed! And I would like to be the next Mayor of Melancholy Falls. Again.

Let the campaign begin!

2
BIG JOAN

The following takes place before Jonathan returns home.

Funny enough, they always called me "Big Joan."

Even though I was born prematurely, and the doctors didn't think I was going to survive...Big Joan was the name that stuck. Probably because, even at that young age, I was a hard-ass. I proved those doctors wrong, and came out on top, despite almost losing my life a number of times during my first few days of living.

Needless to say, I was a bit on the smaller side as a kid. But, someone called me Big Joan as a joke one day, and it just sort of…stuck. Neither one of my parents remembered who actually said it first, but it was a loving moniker given to me by one of them.

I didn't have the easiest of childhoods, given that we weren't actually rolling in money. And I think it goes without saying that I had some health complications growing up. But like I said, I was a fighter, and didn't give up.

My dad always looked out for me. We were two peas in a pod, sometimes almost to the annoyance of my mom. But they both loved me dearly, I know that, and they tried to give me the best life possible. It wasn't always easy, but life sometimes has a way of taking the bad and making it good.

And look at me now…owner of a fine dining establishment, going on our 58th year. We're a Melancholy Falls staple, having been opened by my father back in 1960. I was just a girl when he unlocked the doors for the first time, but I remember it fondly. I sat at the counter, swiveling on one of the stools, and watched as he proudly beamed when the first customers walked in.

Later that night, after he had closed up, he told me he loved visiting diners when he was a kid, and he always wanted one for himself. And there he was, years later, owner of Big Joan's, named as a tribute for his daughter that overcame the odds. If I could do it, so could he; I was his symbol of hope. The diner was almost like my sister in that sense.

I never wanted to run this place, though. Sure, I had fun growing up here, helping my mom and dad where I could. But really…I wanted to paint.

I can't tell you how many times I sat at one of the booths, supplies laid out all over placemats, working on my latest masterpiece. No matter how many I produced, my dad always found a place for it on the walls. At home, at the diner, in relatives' houses, my work wound up everywhere.

When I was in high school, my parents worked hard at the diner in order to make enough to send me to college. Dad didn't fully understand what I could do with an art degree, but he believed in me, and that was enough.

So, away I went. My first semester was great, because it was also my first time out of Melancholy Falls. I had spent my life in this town, so to be able to see the outside, to breathe the air that wasn't located on the Jersey Shore for once…it was exhilarating. Don't get me wrong, I have always loved my home, but I was finally getting to see the world! I was learning things that no book would have been able to teach me, and I was living the life my parents wanted for me.

I even met someone. Charlie was his name. He was a fellow art student, like me. He was from Connecticut, which seemed a world away in my mind. He was sweet, cute, and he was one of the first people to encourage my art. He helped me find new techniques. And after a few weeks, he even told me he loved me, once. And I loved him, too.

Everything was wonderful, and going how I always dreamed my life would.

Until Dad passed away.

It was early in my second semester when my mother called me in tears. Dad didn't come home from the diner one night, so she went to check on him. She found him on the floor. He was breathing, but barely. By the time she got him to the hospital, it was too late. The doctors said it was a heart attack, and she was lucky to have spent his last moments with him. Their words were meant to help, but that didn't comfort her at all.

My dad was gone. He was only 56.

My mom couldn't run Big Joan's by herself, so I came home from college to help. It wasn't meant to be permanent at the time, just for a little while. You know, until things ran smoothly again, and then I would go back to school.

But…that never happened. Things kept piling up, work kept needing to get done, and the extra help we thought we'd have never came through. Charlie was supportive at first, but I wasn't going to make him throw his life away and help me. He had his own art, his own studies, his own life to worry about. The longer I stayed to help, the less he called. Sure enough, the calls stopped coming altogether eventually. I didn't blame him, but that didn't make it sting any less.

My canvases and the brushes went away, and out came the apron and spatula.

Mom wanted me to go back, she even pushed me toward it, but I couldn't leave her alone. Not like that. And after a few years, she passed away, too.

There was no one else left to run the diner…so Big Joan took over.

Sure, I could have sold it, made some money, and went off to live my life. But this place was my father's life. He worked so hard to get it, to make it his own, I couldn't just let it go. I wanted to honor him. So, I stayed. I took on the responsibility, and Big Joan's has been the go-to place in town for years. Mostly because our world famous hot dog platters. And, of course, if you ask any of the regulars, our world famous sass, as well.

I don't keep very many friends these days. It's mostly out of choice, honestly. I work every day, long hours, to keep the diner running. I don't have much time to socialize, beyond what little conversation I have with the customers. The regulars are friendly enough, but you don't see me grabbing a drink with them after work, do you? No, instead I would rather go home, relax, sleep...or paint.

I've never stopped painting, really. My life may not be filled with it like I had originally wanted, but when the quiet moments happen, which are few and far between, I do like to pick up a brush.

It mostly happens late at night. I'll be sleeping, and the urge will strike. I ignored it for the first few years, usually just using my mind to imagine what could have been, but eventually, the need became too strong.

I set up an easel in the attic, next to the window. I'll go up there, around 2 or 3 in the morning, and do a few strokes. I never have a plan, never know what it's going to be, but eventually, something makes itself known on the canvas. A tree filled with birds. A snowy mountain. A lonesome beach, with the sun setting over, casting a gorgeous shade upon it.

Nowadays, the paintings don't get hung up anywhere. They just get piled in the corner. I don't even hang them in my own home, because I have no one to share them with, so why bother? But they are there...out of my head, and onto the canvas. That's all that matters.

I sometimes entertain the idea of going back into it, full-time. Just not showing up at the diner one day, and beginning anew, sharing my talents with the world, somewhere else, far from here. But I could never do that...I could never let my father's legacy go to waste like that. He gave me so much when he was alive, and I still feel like I need to pay him back for it. Maybe one day, I will feel like that debt will be filled, but not yet.

Sometimes I hope for some sort of natural disaster to help speed the process along; maybe there will be an accidental fire, or the roof will collapse. Somewhere where the insurance doesn't cover it all, and it would be too much of a hardship to rebuild. It's a terrible thought, I know...but maybe it's time for me to stop living in the past, and do something for me. Live the life I was meant to, all those years ago.

But until that day...as if it will ever come...here I wait. Grilling burgers, cooking hot dogs, and serving it up with the sass I am known for.

But a woman can dream, can't she?

3
CONFESSIONAL

The following is a transcript of an audio file found on a USB drive that was buried in a lock box in Orange County, California.

Today is March 22nd 1998. This is entry 248 in the confessional of Steven Lundy, First Leading Knight of the Order of Bileth.

This is…very hard for me to do. There is no easy way to do this…I just have to come out and say it.

I killed Tabitha.

She is dead, and it was my doing.

I guess…I should start from the beginning.

There was a period in my life where my father, Christopher Lundy, encouraged me to go out into the world, go to university and learn all the things he'd never had the chance to learn. Despite his wealth, he'd never attended an institute of higher learning. Instead, his father, my grandfather, insisted he stay close to home after completing high school. He wanted him close so he could help with the Order. And, well, Christopher Lundy was unlikely to ever be in need of the gainful employment that university studies would help provide.

But my father wanted me to learn more of the world outside the Order, and university was the place to do that. A broad course of study, he felt, would make me more of a well-rounded leader, when the time came for me to step up and lead. The title of First Leading Knight is earned and not inherited, of course, but there was no question that the title would one day be mine. Even at university, I adored Bileth, lived for Bileth; I inhaled her teachings, and worshipped everything about her.

Until I met Tabitha. Oh…my dear, sweet Tabby.

I met Tabitha during my last year at the university. The moment I laid eyes on her, I knew she was the one for me—I just knew it. And when her piercing eyes fell upon me, I felt a charge course through my body like never before. For years, I had been taught that Bileth touched our hearts in ways that no one else ever could. But Tabitha…in that first moment, she changed my feeling on that. She ensnared my heart as if I were a fox in a trap. Oh, I was helpless…

Weeks had gone by before I had worked up enough courage even to speak to her. And when I did, I fumbled over my words, stuttering, nervousness growing inside. I was a school boy again, the butterflies welling up in my stomach, and fluttering about. I had walked away, thinking myself a fool. Little did I know that she was just as smitten as I…

Our first kiss was three weeks later. Being a proper gentleman, I will spare the sordid details of our youthful exploits, but I will tell you that I had never felt so alive, so free, so full of love. She understood me as no one else ever had. At last, for once, here was someone who knew completely how I felt. And she loved me for it.

In those moments, my heart was filled with Tabby's love…but not Bileth's. I had never meant to neglect her teachings, my faith, my journey toward the One Truth. I had not even realized it was happening myself…that is, until my father appeared at the university one day, and chided me for forgetting Remembrance Day.

Twenty years of my life, and I had never forgotten Remembrance

Day, not once, not ever. But that time, I did. And that was one time too many.

The realization dawned on me…I was slipping away. From Bileth. From her light. From her love. From the Order. My father realized it, too. And with all he had invested in me over the years, there was no way he'd ever allow that to happen. So, I was given an ultimatum.

Either usher Tabitha into Bileth's light…or lose her forever.

Despite our many long hours together, Tabby and me, I had never mentioned to her my unconventional upbringing or my faith. The thought had never even crossed my mind. But, it seemed the time had come to introduce her. Would she take it to heart? Or would she reject the teachings, and force me to make a choice I did not want to make?

It did cross my mind that, if Tabby did not accept Bileth's light…I had no idea how I would react. How much did I love this woman? Did I love her enough to leave behind my faith, my upbringing, my birthright, to live a life with her? A life without Bileth? Would that even be possible? Could I actually do that? Could I turn my back on Bileth, after all the years I had dwelled and flourished in her light?

After much soul searching, much debate, much anguish in myself…I found that, if it came down to it…I believe I could.

Faith is a funny thing for most people. With so many different variations of religions and beliefs in the world, everyone has their own version of what they believe. And when I told Tabby my beliefs, well…I guess it should have come as no surprise to me how well she took to it.

Really, it was like she'd been waiting for something like this to come along, and here it was. I will never forget how she looked at me and said "Steven…with you by my side, I will gladly let Bileth into my heart." It was like we were pieces of a puzzle. She said I completed her. She did. She said I made her feel whole for the first time in her life. Imagine that.

We were married by the year's end. We held a small ceremony before graduation, so my father, who was then in poor health, could see his eldest son married before he passed. The celebration was two-fold: in it, we joined our lives together, and we also joined our lives to Bileth's.

When my father died shortly after, and the title of First Leading Knight fell to me, Tabby was right by my side, as she said she would be. She had learned the teachings and words of Bileth faster than anyone else in the Order ever had, and assisted in the ceremony with complete devotion and joy, as if she was always meant to do so.

Life was good.

And then in 1990, life got even better, when our little Rachel arrived.

We were happy. We were a family. Me. Tabby. And Rachel. All of us bathing in Bileth's light and love. Things were…wonderful.

There is a long pause in the audio file here before it continues.

It was a few years later, when she was out with Rachel, that she had her first episode.

They were at the playground. Tabby dropped her cup of coffee. Suddenly. Without warning. She claimed her hand just fell asleep, and her grip…slipped. When she bent over to clean it up, a dizziness overtook her, and her speech began to slur.

We chalked it up to stress, what with the long nights and days we had been spending, preparing for the Order of Bileth's next phase.

But these…incidents…kept recurring.

Fatigue. Memory disturbances. Trouble walking. Cognitive function…impairments.

The cause of multiple sclerosis is still unknown, but most researchers agree it results from an abnormal response by the body's immune system. This abnormal immune response could be caused by a virus, but it is unlikely just one virus triggers the condition. A normal body usually sends in immune cells to fight off bacteria and viruses; but with multiple sclerosis, those cells misguidedly attack the body's own healthy nervous system. They attack and consume the myelin sheath…the fatty insulation surrounding nerve cells in the brain and spinal cord. Myelin acts like the rubber insulation found in an electric cable, and facilitates the smooth transmissions of messages between the brain, the spinal cord, and the rest of the body. But as the myelin is attacked, the messages are not sent efficiently, and eventually not at all.

The doctors had a regimen they wanted to begin immediately. Life with MS was painful, they claimed, but manageable. Tabitha's life could be extended years, decades even, with their help.

But the Order had other plans.

We have spent our lives, centuries, millennia, trusting in the splendor that is Bileth. Now, there has never been a proscription against the use of traditional Western medicines—help can come from many places—but the Order does frown upon efforts to seek means of healing that go against their ways.

Through Bileth, anything is possible. Through Bileth, your full potential will be unlocked. Through Bileth, your faith will heal you. That is the reward for the strength of your belief: your faith will heal you. Your… faith… will heal you.

And so…against the wishes and determinations of the good doctors, we cast them and their petty remedies aside.

Instead, we prayed. We meditated. With full hearts, we performed the sacred rituals, that we might bring forth Bileth's healing light. We did everything Bileth's teachings decreed for members in our predicament.

It's true that some days were indeed harder than others. Sometimes, Tabitha's condition worsened. But on others, it improved, and those improvements were the proof of our faith. For every bad day, we re-doubled our efforts the next, to show our devotion to Bileth, and to the cause that was greater than either of us. The moments not spent building toward the future of the Order were committed to improving Tabitha's condition. It was not easy for her, but she was brave and devoted. She persisted even as the disease ravaged her body.

In that last year or so, she was confined to her bed; she couldn't stand without assistance. The disease had reduced her by degrees, finally rendering her unable to perform even the simplest of tasks.

But still, no matter the setbacks, no matter how hard it was, no matter how many times we were tested—and I swear, we were tested to the limits of our endurance—we did not waver in our faith.

We knew Bileth had a plan. We knew Bileth would provide. We knew Bileth would save her.

The audio here is unclear. It appears to be a gentle sob before it continues.

She passed this morning. My Tabitha. Almost exactly four years from the day she was diagnosed.

You know, with MS, it's not the disease itself that gets you…it's everything else. It just opens the doors to every other goddamn affliction in the world, and they finish the job.

Like pneumonia.

It was pneumonia.

During her last two weeks in this world, Tabitha couldn't move much in her bed, so it was hard for her to clear her lungs. Me, I could do nothing. Nothing but be there by her side, as she continued to work on the Order's plans, loyal even when she could not do the labor herself.

I held her hand as she took her final breath. She looked at me with those eyes of hers—those eyes—looked into my eyes, all the way down into my soul, the way she did. Then she smiled at me and said, "Bileth…she always finds a way." And that was it…she was gone.

Gone. My Tabby. My dear, sweet Tabby.

And now here I sit, recording my confessional, as the Order's teachings demand. It's what we do when we realize a wrongdoing in our lives and want to clear our conscience of that sin. I have spent too long questioning why, why, why… Why did my Tabitha contract that horrible disease? Why had this pitiless hardship come into our lives? And why, just why did it have to end this way?

And it took me until today to realize that I have no one to blame for it but myself.

Tabitha was put into my life to test my faith, you see…and she was taken from me because I failed that test.

We spent so much of our lives together devoted to the Order, to Bileth herself, but this…disease…was recompense…retribution, even...for that one moment, all those years ago, when I questioned my dedication to Bileth and to the Order. I am punished for my questions then, when, for just the briefest instant, all the world seemed unclear to me, and I did not fully believe in my path. My path. The path down which I had been guided my entire life by Bileth herself, illuminated at every step by her light.

And because Tabitha was the reason for my errant feelings, because she was the reason my love of Bileth faltered in my own heart, because she was the reason I betrayed, for that briefest moment, my own faith…that was why she was stricken with this disease.

Of course she didn't mean to interfere with the path Bileth had destined for me, and of course she couldn't have known that she nearly did lead me astray of the path. But for all that…she had to pay for her sins against Bileth. And for her sins against the First Leading Knight of the Order. But were these her sins, really?

No, no, no, no, they were mine alone. Tabitha paid with her life. But I am punished still. I am the one who must suffer. And prevail.

For my failings, Tabby is dead today. It is my fault. I killed her…because I did not fully trust in Bileth's plan. I will not make that mistake again. Not now, not ever.

For I have felt Bileth's light shine down upon me today, and it has renewed my sense of purpose. It has restored the fullness of my devotion. It has set ablaze the love in my heart. The path before me is clear, as if etched in cold fire at my feet. My eyes are open. My mind is free of obstruction. My vision…is now complete.

I now know the way toward the One Truth, for Bileth has shown me. Her return is nigh upon us, and I shall be the one that leads us there.

My Tabitha may be dead, but she is merely dead…

Bileth…Bileth is not dead, but vibrant and alive in all of us, waiting for her rebirth into this world. Bileth will return. Bileth is coming. She is coming.

And when she does… I know Tabitha will smile upon me for trusting in her plan.

May Bileth's light shine upon you. As it will, I promise, soon shine upon us all.

4
THE DAY AFTER

The following was posted on Tumblr the day after the 2016 Presidential Election.

Buddy woke up to a nightmare. He was sure of it. There was no way it could be true.

But by his second cup of coffee, he could no longer lie to himself. He wasn't still asleep. He wasn't dreaming. He was awake.

It wasn't long before Jonathan roused from his place on the couch. He half-walked, half-stumbled into the kitchen.

"Morning," he managed, while grabbing his own cup.

"Hey," Buddy replied, half-heartedly.

"You doing okay?" Jonathan asked, pouring coffee into his mug, before adding some sugar.

Buddy could only sigh in response, not being able to muster up the words for how he was feeling. He was hurt. Heartbroken. And extremely concerned about the well-being for the future of not just his town, but the entire country.

To Jonathan's credit, he didn't even bother to respond with words; nothing he could have said would have helped, really. Instead, he did the only thing he knew would; he threw his arms around Buddy, embracing him with the biggest hug he'd ever given him.

Buddy returned the gesture, wrapping his arms around his best friend. Both of their tears began to flow freely. The two of them stood there, locked in each other's grip, holding on to each other like nothing else mattered.

Buddy was tired of having to fight for his freedom, for his rights, and he knew that battle just got harder. But he was thankful for Jonathan. For Ami. For everyone who supported him and everyone else in the same situation. They weren't just friends; they were a family.

That hug, that simple gesture, said it all.

They were all in this together. They would fight for what was right.

Love trumps hate. Always.

Be good to each other.

5
HERE COMES…

The follow takes place in 1937.

Edward was dying.

He felt fine, though, as there was nothing physically wrong with him. In fact, he was as healthy as a horse. However, he glanced at the calendar in his kitchen, and checked the date again, hoping it would have magically changed. Of course, it hadn't, and it was still what he feared it to be: April 19, 1937. The date Edward was to die.

He looked at his family, whom were all enjoying a meal around the kitchen table with him. His wife, Margaret, smiled warmly at him. She had made his favorite dinner that evening; sausages with pasta, with that new sauce that had just come out earlier in the year. His youngest daughter, Mary, had come over to join them that evening, while his other two children, James and Elizabeth, were out living their own lives. How he wished he would be able to see them one last time, but alas, that time had passed.

"This is delicious, Margaret, thank you," he said, as he took his last bite. It was serendipitous that she happened to make this meal, his favorite, on this particular night. She didn't know his time was at an end, of course. But through some divine intervention, she blessed him with this final meal.

He wiped his mouth with the napkin that was on his lap, and

stood up from the table.

"Is everything OK, Papa?" Mary asked, a slight look of concern in her eye.

"Yes, fine," he told her reassuringly, and smiled. "Just need some fresh air. I'll be in the yard, if that's alright."

"Take your coat, dear," Margaret told him. "It's a bit chilly this evening."

As he left the kitchen, he made a quick stop at the hallway closet to do just that. He was already a bit chilled to the bone, but not because of the weather. However, he did feel a bit warmer after he put on his coat.

His backyard was modest, but it was enough for him. In fact, many of the other homes there in Orange, NJ were the same. Modest, single family dwellings that people moved into to spend the rest of their days.

In the back corner of the yard was a small shed, one that doubled as Edward's "office," and that is where he went. Aside from a few gardening tools, and the mower that Margaret insisted he purchase last summer, it was mostly his sanctuary away from the rest of the world. A small desk, with two chairs on opposite sides, took up most of the room.

This very desk had been in his possession for many years. It held great sentimental value to him. Though he hadn't sung in some time, he had spent many nights hunched over that desk, writing new lyrics, while someone sat opposite, figuring out the melody. It served him well. But, these days, it mostly served as a nice, quiet place for him to unwind and listen to records from the old days, courtesy of the phonograph that sat on top of it.

There was a single candle, the only light source in the room, that also sat on the desk. As Edward closed the door to the shed, shutting out the outside, he sat down in one of the chairs, and lit the candle. As soon as the flame sprang to life, Edward noticed he wasn't alone.

Sitting in the chair opposite him, on the other side of the desk, was the man he was dreading to see.

"Comment vas-tu, mon cher?" he asked, smoking a cigarillo, a small pillar of smoke coming off its tip.

"Those things will kill you, don't you know that?" Edward replied, not even sure it would make a difference. "And you nearly scared me half to death."

"Oh, my dear Edward, how much easier that would have made my job."

Edward slunk back into his chair, knowing his end was near. DW's devilish smile was illuminated by the candle, his eyes looking directly into Edward's soul.

"But...that would have taken the fun out of it, no?" DW said.

"I suppose it's time then?" Edward asked, lighting up one of the cigarettes he kept hidden in the desk drawer. They were secreted away there mostly because he told Margaret he stopped smoking years ago.

DW's grin merely grew wider, as he reached into his black coat and pulled out a pocket watch. He opened it, its silver casing glinting in the candle light, and studied it. After a moment, he glanced back at Edward, the smile never leaving his face.

"Just about," DW said, taking another puff of his cigarillo. He gently blew the smoke across toward Edward.

"You're a real son of a bitch, you know that?" Edward shot back, waving the vapor away from his face.

"Oh, I'm the son of a bitch?" DW laughed. "Lest we forget how we came to this, but no, I am always the one to blame. Funny how that works out, isn't it?"

Edward didn't need reminding; the situation had been replaying, clear as day, over and over in his head, for the last several weeks.

It was all Ada's fault, honestly. She was the one to blame. If she had just taken the offer, like he wanted, none of this would have happened. But no...she was too spoiled for that. Too "famous."

They had worked together only once, and it went well enough. They recorded one of Edward's songs, one he adapted from a poem, as a parable between the ragged and the naive. Though she was over 40 at the time, Ada's vocals as the young girl added a bit more to the song, giving it the breath of life needed. It became a semi-success in 1919, selling a whole slew of Edison records that it was recorded on.

Edward did well enough, of course, but he never had the sort of career Ada had. He sold out a few gigs in Atlantic City, but never to the crowds that she got. If only he could work with her again, maybe play a few shows together, he was sure he would get the recognition he deserved. However, she refuted him. She had her own career, that selfish cow, and claimed she didn't particularly enjoy working with Edward to begin with.

He tried, again and again, but each time she refused. The final time was when he made a special trip to see her at her home in North Carolina back in 1922. Instead of appreciating the gesture, having made such a long journey to see her, she lashed out, and called him pathetic.

Something inside Edward snapped then. He wasn't sure what happened, his mind seemed to have blocked it out. But when he came back to reality, he was standing over Ada Jones' body...a bloodied rag stuffed in her mouth.

He panicked, unsure of what exactly transpired. He was certain that he was going to spend the rest of his days behind bars.

But then, seemingly out of nowhere, DW appeared, and made him an offer that he couldn't refuse. He slinked over the body, examining Edward's handiwork, and smiled that devilish grin that Edward came to despise.

"I will clean up this mess, and you won't have a care in the world about it...in exchange for your services, upon the contract's completion, of course," DW told him. He wasn't exactly sure what his 'services' were to be, but he didn't care. A date was set, and Edward shook his hand, right then and there… and almost immediately regretted it.

Kidney failure was the official story for Ada's passing, and what was on her death certificate. But that didn't stop the rumors from circulating. People talked in hushed whispers that Edward was indeed the last person to see her alive, but beyond that, it was all speculation. Kidney failure was on the official report, and so kidney failure was what everyone believed.

Mostly.

Edward's career mostly stayed the same after that, working when he could, but it never really took off like he wanted it to. At first, he blamed it on his deal with DW.

But soon, he just forgot all about it. He didn't see DW at all, so he hoped that maybe, just maybe, he forgot about it also. He almost believed this day would never come. But as the days grew close to April 19, 1937, it all began to come back to him.

And now, DW sat before him, smiling and smoking, his gaze never leaving Edward.

"There isn't anything I can do?" Edward practically pleaded with him.

"Haven't you done enough already?" DW replied.

Edward hung his head, almost in shame, knowing that there was no real way out of it.

"What's going to happen to me?"

"Oh, you know. A little of this...a little of that." DW got up from his chair, and dropped his cigarillo to the ground, stomping out its tiny flame. He walked over to a cabinet on the far side of the shed, and began to go through its contents. "The exact details you don't need to be privy to, but essentially...well, those undeserving better beware."

"So, what...I'll be in your control?" Edward inquired.

"Yes...and no. Let's just say I'm making a few changes in my life, but I need someone to follow in my stead," DW replied cryptically.

"Does that mean I'm going to be a devil now?"

"You should be so lucky," DW laughed.

"And my family?"

"They'll be fine. Sad, of course, that their patriarch has passed, but no harm will come to them."

"Do you promise?"

DW stopped, and looked at Edward, feigning offense. He scoffed before answering.

"You have my word, mon cher," he replied. "A deal's a deal, and the deal is only for you."

"What happens now, then?"

DW eventually selected a record from the cabinet's depths. He showed it to Edward, smiling as he did.

"Appropriate choice, don't you think?"

Edward knew his choice wasn't coincidence. The record he held up was none other than the one and only song he did with Ada Jones: The Raggity Man.

With an air of grace, DW came back over to the desk, and placed the record on the phonograph. Within moments, its haunting melody began to play. Edward leaned back, and listened. It was still one of his favorites, despite the tragedy that went along with it.

"I'm sorry for what I did, if that's any consolation," Edward confided. "I didn't mean for that to happen. It just...did."

"I know, I know," DW told him. "You'll get no judgements from me. I merely gave you a second chance, to try to live the life you wanted...for a little while, at least. But the question remains...was it worth it, Edward? Did you do everything with that extra time that you wanted?"

Edward thought of his wife, Margaret, and how in love with her he still was. He thought of his children; how he was able to see them grow up, and start families of their own. He thought of the life he lived, and while not perfect in any sense, he did the best he could with what he had. He loved his family. He loved his life.

He made peace with the fact that it was all over now.

"Yes," he told the devil that stood before him. "Yes, it was worth every moment. Thank you."

DW smiled, the first genuine one that Edward had ever seen him do.

*Here comes that Raggity Man, with his rags, rags, rags...*the record player sang sweetly. Edward's own voice from the past filling the shed, as DW crept up behind him.

Edward braced himself for the pain that would surely follow shortly afterward. But instead, DW gently placed his hands upon his shoulders, steadying him.

"This song...it's your calling card, Edward. Your legacy. And from now on, whenever this record is played...you will find the unworthy and punish them, to make up for your one, selfish act, all those years ago. Do you understand?"

He nodded his head, tears welling in his eyes.

"I can sense the remorse in you, rolling off in waves. However, I'm feeling a bit...generous today," DW told him. "You caught me on a good day, so hear this: I will amend your contract to include a single stipulation, to perhaps shorten your sentence in my service. You will continue to be this avatar of judgement for as long as these records exist."

DW motioned toward the phonograph, still spinning and playing the song.

"When every, last copy has been destroyed...only then will you be released. Your greatest triumph must be erased in order to set you free. That is my gift to you...my Raggity Man."

Edward nodded again, the tears coming faster now.

"Thank you..." was all he managed to get out.

"It's time, Edward."

Edward closed his eyes.

He was ready.

6

WOMAN OF THE FALLS

The following is an excerpt taken from pages 437-440 of *Built on the Foundations of Madness: A Brief History of Melancholy Falls' Origins, Local Legends, and More* by Franklin McCraney Jr, c. 1972

Ever since the city was founded in 1647, the waterfall, located in Newbold Woods on the East side of town, has been the center of much speculation. Though the origins of naming it 'Melancholy Falls' have often been debated, what is widely known is the tragic history it shares. Long before our forefathers settled here, the falls were considered a place of dread by the original inhabitants of the area.

Their legends told of an ancient creature living just behind the curtain of the falls, luring unsuspecting victims to its lair as tragedy befell them in some way. While the creature has been called many things over the years, the most common name for it is the 'Woman of the Falls.'

While our town founders searched for the perfect land to settle upon, they were warned to stay far from this place by the local Lenni Lenape tribe. It was only after one of the settling party, a young woman by the name of Jessica Fieldlin, wandered away from the group that the falls were discovered. As the evening drew long, and she had still not returned to her family, a search party went out to find her. It wasn't long before they came upon the falls proper, along with Fieldin's body, broken and battered at the base of the falls.

It was believed that she had slipped and fell to her death. However, her misfortune was also considered a boon for the settlers, as they found the land upon which the town was founded. To honor her, and to remember their loss, they named both the water feature and the town Melancholy Falls, for even though they were glad to have found somewhere to live, it was marred by tragedy.

Over the years, the falls have been the center of controversy, as many have lost their lives there. Though most of these have been deemed accidents, there have been many recorded incidents where the lines between fiction and reality have been blurred.

For example, in September 1682, Melancholy Falls' first mayor, Rutherford DePalma (the first in a long line of DePalmas to inhabit that role), wrote in the official township journal of an occurrence he experienced while fishing at the falls. He and some companions (unnamed in the entry) were at the base of the falls, where '*...the water rages the hardest upon its descent from the fall itself.*' Though they had fished in this spot before, on multiple occasions, this was the first time something strange occurred.

DePalma writes:

It was upon the second fish being placed in our fishing basket that we noticed a strange humming noise. Whilst the noise was low at first, it soon turned into what we perceived to be a female voice singing a melody. Only males were present in the vicinity, so we initially took it to be someone above us, perhaps playing with friends. However, a woman with golden hair soon appeared from behind the falls itself. While we could not make out her form completely, as she was obscured by the rushing water, there was no doubt the singing was coming from her direction.

As the entry goes on, one of their party tried to make his way behind the falls to find the young woman, but it proved too much for him. He went under the water within moments, and was lost. While an attempt was made to recover him by DePalma and his associates, it proved fruitless, and he was deemed deceased.

Alas, the female form and the singing also disappeared after the brave young man did, and the group was left alone. While the loss of a fellow man was very real, they believed the vision of a woman to be a group hallucination…but thought enough of it to record it in official town records.

While there many, similar instances such as DePalma's account, the next one of real significance happened in 1832. During this account, Jacqueline Maddox, 17, relates how her potential suitor, Bartholomew Colby, 19, met an untimely end.

While it is believed that Colby took Maddox to the falls in attempts to woo and, perhaps, even propose to her, their story took a much darker turn. After a picnic lunch, yet again, at the base of the falls, Colby became distracted by a singing female who he believed to be behind the falls.

Maddox's statements from the official report:

Bartholomew took it upon himself to explore, as he felt that someone might be in trouble. He skirted the area beneath the waterfall to get behind it (EDITOR'S NOTE: At this point in the town's history, a makeshift path had been created to reach the underside of the waterfall, allowing easier access. Who, or what, made said path is unknown). I called out to him a number of times, but received no response. Fearing the worst, I hitched up my skirt and followed after him. The path was slippery, but manageable. However, once I made my way to the backside, I found myself in a cave. I had no recollection or memory of it ever being there before, but there it was. I heard a horrible noise from deep within it, and against my better judgement, followed the sounds deeper into the cave.

After turning around a bend, there was a small alcove that was as big as a large room. Candles lined the walls, and illuminated the darkness. But of more concern was what was causing the noise I had earlier heard; a young blonde woman, completely nude, had her face in Bartholomew's neck. While I had originally thought I had stumbled upon some lewd act, I saw Bartholomew reach out toward me. It was then that the woman turned. Her face was twisted into a scowl of hatred, and her mouth was covered in blood. Bartholomew's neck was from whence said blood came, as she had been chewing through it. I screamed and ran out of there as quickly as I could. I could not remember my journey back into town, but they tell me I came screaming out of the woods, and would not stop until someone calmed me down.

Again, a search party was formed, but young Master Colby's body was never recovered. However, many believe that Miss Maddox was actually the cause of Colby's demise, and that she concocted this wild story to shift the blame elsewhere. Maddox was never convicted of the crime, but lived with the grief of what transpired. She was committed to a mental institution years later, where the memory of that day still haunted her.

While we must take Maddox's story with a grain of salt, it is worth noting that this is the first time we have any concrete description of the 'creature' beneath the falls, and thus, must enter it into our history. Every instance before this one was met with vague generalities, not giving more details than just a 'woman' and a 'singing voice.' This story is the very first time where a more definitive look is given...and one that plays into later tales of said creature.

These sorts of encounters persist throughout the rest of the 19th century, and early into our own. The so-called 'Woman of the Falls' is the most prevalent tall tale in our town's history, and questions raised by it might never have an answer. Its origins could be simple superstition, rooting back to when Jessica Fieldlin lost her life to give birth to the town. However, as noted before that, legends from local tribes existed long before that incident.

While the Lenni Lenape are not known to have written vast accounts of their history, they are oral storytellers. Long has passed since this story was originally told, so its original form is surely muddled. But, here it is, as best as I can recount the pieces told to me over the years.

According to their beliefs, the creature once roamed the Earth, causing misery and destruction wherever it passed. Often taking the form of a young woman, she would lure unsuspecting victims into her traps before feasting upon their still beating hearts. The Lenape lost a great number of their tribe to her, as she wandered the New Jersey wilds. One day, a brave warrior from their numbers vowed to put a stop to it. Legend has it that he enlisted the help of a medicine woman, once banished from the Lenape tribe, but knowledgeable in the darker magics needed to stop this creature.

Acting as a wounded man, the warrior managed to lure the creature to the cave hidden behind the falls. As she was about to pounce on her prey, the warrior leapt into action, piercing its side with his spear, and pinning it against a nearby cave wall. As the medicine woman came from the shadows to begin her work, the creature supposedly transformed into a beautiful, young woman before their very eyes, pleading with them to let her go. But, they were both prepared for such trickery, and ignored her cries.

While the pair were unable to completely banish the creature, as was their plan, they were able to trap it within the falls. The cave behind the falls was to be its final resting place. When all was said and done, the Lenni Lenape played it safe, and avoided the area at all costs, so they would never have to encounter the creature again. Of course, such a story has never been verified, but it does align with the sightings of the 'beautiful woman' that take place in the area surrounding the falls over the years, and thus, the likely culprit for this local legend.

While no official record has been made to map out the underground cave system beneath the town, there is a small chance that the one beneath the falls is connected in some way. However, as we have learned during the mine collapse of 1941, such caves are unstable, and thus, too dangerous to explore.

Perhaps some time in the future, brave souls will chart the area, and maybe, just maybe, come face to face with the 'Woman of the Falls' herself.

7

"ARE YOU KIDDING ME?!"

The following takes place after Former Mayor DePalma's speech in front of City Hall earlier this week.

The voice, like nails on a chalkboard, screeched out from the innermost office within City Hall. Sharon should have been used to it by now, but no matter how many times there was an outburst during her time as an intern, it always caught her by surprise. She glanced at the clock on the wall to her left, and took note of the time. It was 11:37AM, and in five seconds, there would be a crash.

Sure enough, in exactly five seconds, something shattered against a wall in the other room. Bracing herself for the inevitable finale of this eruption of anger, Sharon did her best not to look at the wall to her right. She counted down another five seconds, and as reliable as Old Faithful, Mayor Norma Jean May came rampaging through the wall that separated her office from Sharon's work space.

When a normal person has a rage-filled episode, they often burst through doors, slamming them open like some sort of angry Kool-Aid Man. Though the Mayor was currently the same color as him, that was where the similarities ended.

Mayor Norma Jean wasn't like normal people, mostly because she wasn't even 'people' any longer; she was a non-corporeal, vengeful wraith. And when one is non-corporeal, there is no need for doors when you can just phase right through walls to get to where you need to be.

That wasn't the same for her aide, though, as Mr. Plickens did have to use the door, and did just that, as he followed Mayor Norma Jean into Sharon's area.

"Plickens!" Mayor Norma Jean bellowed, as she pointed to the coffee mug on the edge of Sharon's desk. Mr. Plickens picked it up and tossed it across the room without hesitation, smashing it into a thousand tiny shards against the far wall.

It always made Sharon laugh that, since the Mayor was non-corporeal, she had to have someone else throw things in a fit of rage for her. However, she did her best to stifle her smile.

"Norma Jean, please, let's take a moment to..." Mr. Plickens began as soon as the debris settled, but he was unable to finish, because Mayor Norma Jean lifted him up by his shirt collar, and that shut up him quickly.

"Plickens," Mayor Norma Jean raged, "If you tell me to calm down again, I will throw you from a third story window, and watch as the birds feast upon your split open head. Understood?" Mr. Plickens nodded as best he could, as he was dropped to the floor.

While this was happening, Sharon continued to stare at her computer screen, desperately trying to look like she was working, but failing miserably. Much like a mood ring, Mayor Norma Jean's transparent color changed from crimson red to a more reasonable white as she floated down to Sharon's level, and smiled politely.

"Sharon, dear," she inquired pleasantly, despite her rage just moments ago. "Have you seen the news yet?" Sharon put on her best fake smile, and looked at her boss.

"No, ma'am, I haven't. Is something wrong?" she asked, knowing full well that something was indeed wrong.

"Well, my sweet," Mayor Norma Jean began, caressing Sharon's face as best as one without corporeal fingers could caress someone's face, "It seems as if former Mayor DePalma is no longer indisposed."

A smile crossed Sharon's face, as she thought this was wonderful news.

"Oh, this is wonderful news!" she exclaimed, but her smile quickly faded as she saw Mayor Norma Jean's color get flush again. Fearing retaliation, Sharon shrunk backward in her chair as best she could, but thankfully, the Mayor seemed to control her rage enough to return back to her normal, white, transparent color.

"Why, yes, that is excellent for her," Mayor Norma Jean said. "We're all very happy for her here at City Hall. However...she has announced that she is running for office, and wants to unseat me in a special election. Now, as understanding as I am to this town's stance on special elections, as it was what got me elected in the first place, you do see how this creates a problem for me, yes?"

Sharon nodded yes. Of course she understood. But would having former Mayor DePalma back in office be so bad?

"So, you understand how having Mayor DePalma back in office would be bad? Not just for me...but the entire City Hall staff?"

Sharon nodded again. When Mayor Norma Jean came on, she replaced most of the staff, except for the elected officials of the City Council, with her own people. Sharon herself was brought on shortly after Mayor Norma Jean came into office, having applied for the position to fulfill a political science credit at Melancholy Falls University.

"Of course, that means, we must do everything we can to make sure she doesn't win, yes?" Mayor Norma Jean asked.

Sharon debated this question for half a second, but in the end, nodded her head again. She didn't want to, at best, further upset the Mayor, or, at worst, be the focus of her rage. However, she had a sinking feeling about where this conversation was headed.

"I think you know where this is headed," Mayor Norma Jean said, floating just above Sharon now, towering over her in an attempt to look intimidating. Truth be told, it worked, especially in light of what the Mayor was about to request.

You see, when Sharon took this job, she was careful to look over all the job duties before officially accepting. At a glance, everything was in order and seemed fairly normal. As most job descriptions do, there was a section toward the end that read 'other duties as needed.' For other jobs, this section generally included things such as 'working an extra hour to complete a project' or 'helping someone in another department get a form' or even 'driving the boss to get their car from Jerry the mechanic.' However, as an intern working directly for the Mayor of Melancholy Falls (who also happened to be a non-corporeal being), 'other duties as needed' went quite a bit further than that.

"I need to borrow your skin suit for a bit, Sharon," the Mayor said. "I need to run some errands to help ensure victory for our side."

Despite the indelicate way of her phrasing, this was a very delicate topic for Sharon. The Mayor wanted to possess her body, and take control, in order to do whatever it was she needed to do.

A year ago, when Sharon first began working there, the request seemed benign enough. The Mayor said it was for the good of the town, and promised to take good care of her body. Though an unusual request, Sharon believed in Mayor Norma Jean, and agreed with very little convincing needed. She awoke, hours later, at home in her own bed, with no recollection of what the Mayor had done while in control, but happy to help the town she loved so dearly.

The request came in every few weeks, and Sharon was always too happy to oblige…until she began to hear rumors of just what the Mayor was up to. Of course, she never had any official confirmation, but the more she thought on it, the less she felt comfortable allowing someone else to run rampant in her body.

See, the thing of it was that in order for Mayor Norma Jean to take control, Sharon had to agree. And Sharon swore to herself that the next time the Mayor asked, she would not agree. She would stand up to her, despite how terrifying she could be when she was angry. The time to do so was now. She had to tell her no.

"No," Sharon uttered softly, the sound barely escaping her lips. Mayor Norma Jean smiled, and looked deep into Sharon's eyes.

"I'm sorry, my dear...I think I may have been distracted by all of this craziness with Mayor DePalma," said the Mayor. "But for a moment, it sounded like you said 'no.' Surely, that's not what you said, yes?"

Sharon stood up from her chair, and looked back at the Mayor, trying to stare her down as much as one could stare someone down while they were floating above your head.

"No," she said again. "No, you may not take control of my body."

There was a moment where nothing happened. A pin drop would have been deafening in the silence. But then, the hair on the back of Sharon's neck stood up. A slight electrical charge slowly filled the room. Mr. Plickens crawled to safety behind one of the visitor chairs by Sharon's desk. Mayor Norma Jean turned a deeper color of red than Sharon ever thought possible.

"...no?" the Mayor questioned.

"No?" she asked again.

"NO?!" she exploded in a fury unlike anyone had ever seen. A black cloud filled the top of the room, lightning bolts and fury emanating from it.

"How dare you..." Mayor Norma Jean began.

"How dare *you*!" Sharon cut her off, surprising everyone, including herself, by the sudden outburst. The Mayor was so taken aback by this that she took a step back. Or, rather, she floated back a step.

"This has gone on long enough!" Sharon said. "You have used and abused me for far too long, and the possession of my body goes well beyond normal work place job responsibilities! I have researched it, and trust me, and bodily possession is not covered under any applicable laws."

She had never spoken to her boss in such a way before, always being too terrified to do so. But she couldn't contain it now, it just coming off of her in waves. And honestly, it felt...good.

"You dare speak to me in such a manner?" the Mayor raged. "After providing you a job for so long?"

"I don't even get paid for this!" Sharon retorted. "I get credits for a college class, not a cushy government salary and pension plan! You should be treating me with respect, not using me for nefarious actions!"

The storm cloud above grew darker, as lightning flashed around the room, growing with Norma Jean's rage.

"You ungrateful little whelp," the Mayor screamed. "You are lucky that I don't..."

"Don't what?" Sharon cut her off again. "Demand Plickens to throw something across the room for you? Face it, Norma, you're not as powerful as you want everyone to believe."

As if the talking back wasn't enough, calling the Mayor simply 'Norma' was definitely the move that caused her to blow her top. Everyone knew it was ALWAYS 'Norma Jean' or 'Mayor Norma Jean' or something along those lines. Never was she to be called just 'Norma.' That was just inviting disaster.

"ARE YOU KIDDING ME?!" the Mayor bellowed, the entire room shaking with her fury. Mr. Plickens cowered in the corner, trying to hide his face as best he could, shielding himself from her wraith.

"I'm not," Sharon said calmly, taking all this surprisingly well. "In fact, I quit." She picked up her purse, and took a step toward the door.

"You can't QUIT!" the Mayor raged. "Because I am FIRING YOU!"

"It's too late for that, Norma, I already quit. You can't fire someone who no longer works for you," Sharon said, her hand on the door knob.

"And where do you think you will go?!" Mayor Norma Jean asked smugly. "Who will hire you without a recommendation from me? Face it, your political career is over unless you stick with me!"

Sharon thought on this for a moment before a revelation came to her in a flash.

"I'm sure the DePalma team would like to know how the Norma Jean administration is run," Sharon said with a smile as she opened the door, walking out on her former life and toward her new one.

8
DEATH TAKES A HOLIDAY

The following takes place after the djinn's attack on Melancholy Falls.

Something isn't right in Melancholy Falls.

That isn't hyperbole, it is a fact. Something is off.

For the many hundreds of years she had been doing her job, she had never encountered a problem such as this. The balance must not be thrown off, so she had decided to investigate it for herself as opposed to sending one of her subordinates. Some jobs just required the finesse of the boss in order to get done. That, and she didn't really want anyone else to know about it yet.

Especially those whom were considered her direct superiors.

People have had many stories about her over the years, and while most are true, the one that isn't is that she has always been the same person. That's just ridiculous to think about, honestly. I mean, who wants to be Death for all of eternity?

So, yes, she was not the first. In fact, she wasn't even the second, third, or fourth. She was just one of many in the long, long line of those who have been Death before her. But when she inherited the role, she gained the first-hand knowledge of all those whom held position previously. Every single instance, encounter, and soul they had taken to the other side, she knew all the intimate details about.

But not this. This was the first time that something like this had ever come up.

The first time it happened, she ignored it.

People die and come back from the other side all the time. That's why they call them 'near death experiences.' Usually it's just for a few minutes, at the most, but there have been some rare cases of people coming back after hours or even days. Reports were filed, of course, but all were deemed normal circumstances, and were left well even alone. She knew this to be true because had checked the files, and believe you me, that was a lot of paperwork to go through.

But for someone to die, come back, then die again, and then come back a second time? That warranted her personal attention.

And so, that was how Death wound up stalking the streets of Melancholy Falls; the twice death and twice re-birth of the man called Zayne Sanguine.

Not wanting to cause any panic or worry (or, like mentioned before, alert her superiors to a problem), she decided to keep this low-key. Instead of opening an official investigation, she simply put in a request to take a few personal days. She had plenty of banked PTO time, considering she had never taken time off before, so it was approved without hesitation. All things considered, this was her first official "vacation" since her civilian life.

She may be in town for work, but she would be damned if she wasn't going to try to relax, too.

But as soon as she arrived, she got that feeling; the one that raised the hairs on the back of her neck, her arms, and even her legs. Something wasn't right in Melancholy Falls...and it went well beyond the resurrections of Mr. Sanguine.

The air was different here, she noticed. It felt heavier, in some ways, and carried an almost copper taste to it. She had experienced similar sensations before, like among the streets of Pompeii before the eruption and in England during the Middle Ages. But this one was worse for some reason. The stench of impending disaster always lingered in places where it was to happen, but it was never as overpowering as this. It made her eyes water, and her knees weak.

After she checked into her room at the Melancholy Motor Inn Motel, she laid back on the all-too-soft mattress, and closed her eyes. She fell asleep swiftly, not realizing how tired she actually was.

She dreamt of her life; not of what she was before Death, but what she had become after. She remembered little of her life as a human, and didn't consider her life to have really begun until she began to work for Afterlife LLC. Of course, it didn't have that name then; that came later, during the 20th century, to make things fit in with the modern world. Back when she joined, it was just a nebulous conglomerate organization, one that had been running for millennia (and would continue to do so, well after her time).

She dreamt of her own death, in which the only memories she had of it were extremely bright lights and a searing pain. Beyond that, there was the vast nothingness of the Void, and then...Death's warm embrace.

Death welcomed her into the fold, inviting her to become one of his 'minions,' as he called it. The minions did the majority of Death's so-called dirty work, while Death oversaw the entire operation. Of course, he still got his hands dirty, when the time was needed, but ultimately, he was the man behind the curtain.

She wasn't sure why she was chosen for this task; she wasn't even sure that she cared. But she was chosen, and that is what mattered.

She took pride in her job, and did it with zest. She helped bring those whose lives were at an end to the other side, and did so with more caring than most. This did not go unnoticed, so when Death announced his retirement, she became the frontrunner to take on the mantle.

She dreamt of her time in the role: the failures, the triumphs, and everything in between.

She dreamt until a knock on the door awoke her.

She sat up immediately. Only slightly disoriented, it took a moment to remember where she was. She blinked sleep from her ancient eyes as the knock returned again, startling her. She looked to the door, studying it.

Who knew she was here? She hadn't made any of her superiors or subordinates aware of her plans, nor would they violate the homing protocol unless of a severe emergency (and she would have felt it if there was one of those).

She got up from the bed, and made her way to the door. She didn't look out the peep hole, but instead, pressed her ear against the wood. Sometimes, you saw more if you didn't use your eyes. That was the only reason she wasn't startled when the knock came a third time; she heard it coming.

"Can I help you?" she rasped out, using her speaking voice for the first time in what seemed liked ages. She cleared her throat, clearing away the years of non-use, before calling out again. "I didn't ask for any towels."

"Nor am I bringing you any," came the voice from the other side. It was a man's voice, one that she was already familiar with, even if they had never met in person. She hesitated a moment, but ultimately decided to open the door. By the time it was fully open, she was wearing her most welcoming smile, the one that had comforted so many in their final moments.

"What a pleasant surprise to see you," she said. "It's not often one comes seeking *me* out before I come for them."

"Though I imagine that's why you are here," Zayne said, doing his best to avoid her gaze directly, instead directing his sight line elsewhere. Humans always had trouble looking her directly in the eyes, almost as if they could see things in them that they didn't want to see.

"Won't you come in?" she asked him, taking a step back to allow him entrance. He nodded in appreciation, and entered. She offered him the chair, the only seat in the room (though there was no desk, so it seemed pointless to even be there to begin with), and he took it. When he had settled, she sat on the bed again, facing him.

Both sat in silence for a few moments. Neither was in a rush to begin the conversation.

"I imagine you know who I am," she eventually said, breaking the stillness between them.

"Yes," he said at once. "And forgive me for not paying proper respects earlier. It is an honor to meet you." He bowed his head in consideration, though she motioned for him to stop.

"Please, none of that. I'm not here on business. I'm here for me. Which...how did you find me?" she asked, genuinely curious.

"Methods which I am not proud of, I assure you. But alas...I knew, and so I came," he replied. He even looked sorry while he said so, which seemed most unusual for him.

"You know why I am here then?" she asked. He merely nodded this time.

"It is most unusual, your situation," she continued. "You have passed the veil not just once, but twice, and both times have returned to the land of the living. Both instances were technically considered your 'time' and yet, my records indicate otherwise now. How is this possible?"

"It is hard to explain," he began, not really intending to go on beyond that. "It would take years for a lesser being such as myself to disclose the situation to its full intent."

"I have the time," she replied, her smile showing that she intended to wait if need be. Zayne sighed.

"With respect, there are forces at work here beyond even you, ma'am," he said.

"There are no forces beyond death," she told him. "And I do not mean Death, as in my title. I mean death, as in the act. Everything succumbs to it in the end. There is no escape." And she believed that. Her superiors may be above her, but even they had to answer to death in the end, didn't they?

"While that may be true, some of those rules of old no longer apply here," he told her. "I have work yet to do, and so, I was brought back."

"Twice," she corrected him. "An anomaly I am unable to explain or account for. Hence my presence."

"All in due time. But I am afraid I am not at liberty to discuss, even with you, unfortunately."

She understood his stance. Despite reading his entire file, front to back, multiple times, she felt she couldn't get a real feel as to who he was. That was, until he was standing before her. One of her talents was being able to read people, and at a glance, tell just what type a person someone was within moments. She was reading him now, and saw a man in conflict. He was at a crossroads in his life, bound by duty and his own moral compass. However, he tried his best to contain that inside…but nothing can hide from Death.

"You're conflicted," she told him. It wasn't a question, it was a statement. One that shook him to his core. For the first time since he entered the room, he looked her directly in the eyes. She saw him for what he truly was, beyond the facade that he haphazardly constructed around himself. She found the truth within him.

Death had no power over your destiny unless it was your time to go. And as much as she searched his soul, she could tell it wasn't his yet...despite the fact that he had already passed over twice.

Their gaze was locked for several moments, neither wanting to look away. When he still didn't speak, she spoke for him.

"You're unsure of your path, of the choices you have made, of the way you have aligned yourself," she said softly. "I have seen inside your heart, Zayne Sanguine. And while I cannot see the future, when the time comes, you will make the right choice. That I know to be true."

Zayne's shoulder's slumped, as if a huge weight was lifted off of him. He looked down at the carpet, collecting himself as best he could.

"Thank you," was all he was able to mutter, before looking at her again.

"You won't try to take me again, will you?" he asked.

"No," she told him. She meant it, too. She wouldn't even attempt it, as The Forces That Were And Always Will Be marked this man's time as not at its end. For now.

"But I will find out why eventually. And when your time comes...I will be there to see you through it," she said. She smiled at him again. "Death can be understanding...when time allows it to be."

He stood from the chair, and made his way to the door. He gripped the handle, and only opened it halfway before he stopped.

"I hope to see you again someday, Celia," he said, before he walked out the door and shut it behind him. As he left, she thought she saw tears in his eyes. Even though the door was shut, she watched him go in her mind's eye.

How curious, she thought. Why had he called her Celia? Did he mistake her for someone else? Or was there something more...

That was of no matter now. Instead, she laid back on the bed and closed her eyes. Within moments, she was sleeping again.

She dreamt of her life. Her death.

And when she awoke in the morning...she remembered.

9
THE NEVER-WAS

It is unsure when the following takes place.

It sat in the dark, and waited.

There was no beginning, no end, not even a middle to its existence. It just simply was.

Being trapped between worlds was hardly an existence, though. How could something be if it stayed in this place where nothing should survive? It reality, it wasn't 'simply was.'

It Never-Was.

Its origins were unknown even to it, its purpose still a mystery. But it was alive, as anything could be in this place, and it waited.

Time meant nothing here.

The place between the worlds was filled with a vast array of Nothingness. On either side, different planes of existence go on, unknowing how close they are to each other, how thin the membrane dividing them actually is. The Nothingness stretched on for miles, millennia, and no end was ever in sight.

The Never-Was walked, and with no sun, no moon, it could journey for days at a time. It often did. It explored this Nothingness.

It catalogued its findings, filing them away in a brain that should not exist, but yet, still filled with thoughts, ambitions…and hunger.

It was this hunger that filled it, just as it had for as long as it existed, as it bode its time. The hunger often led to the Place.

This Place was unlike the rest of the Nothingness. Whereas everything there was nothing, here, there was something.

The walls here were thin, yes, but impenetrable. But at this Place, there was a single, tiny crack. The Never-Was found it by accident, after years and years of missing it completely. But now that it knew it was there, it was drawn to it, again and again. Whenever it was far, the hunger grew in unfathomable ways. But when it was near, the hunger sated. Something called out to it from here. In a place where Nothingness abounded, it would return to this Place, just to feel...something.

Overtime, that was no longer enough.

It began to scratch at the crack in the walls. It cannot be known how long it had worked at it. It cannot be known when it first began to notice progress. It is only known that the Never-Was was taking that tiny crack and making it larger. It did this whenever it could, whenever it would pass by this Place. The feeling of something grew as each bit of the wall was chipped away.

Millennia passed.

And when it did, the Never-Was could begin to see through to the other side. In a world of darkness, where it knew nothing else, the light that began to emanate from the other side was unlike anything it had ever seen.

It wanted more.

It did not understand what it saw, but the hunger inside began to grow again. But the light, the one that shone from that Other Place, was the answer. That was the key to ending its hunger. It didn't know how it knew that, it just did.

And so, it continued its work. It was slow going, but the more it scratched, the clearer the image on the other side became. The light was almost unbearable now, but it did not give up its task.

As it continued its work, a single word formed in its mind. It didn't know the meaning of this word, nor that it was even a word to begin with. But it knew this word was the source of the light it so craved, the answer to its problem, the end of its hunger.

If only it could get to it, consume it, and whatever controlled it…

The word was a simple one: talisman.

The Never-Was was almost through.

10
ONE MORE

The following takes place shortly before the confrontation with the Jersey Devil.

Hey, bartender, can I have another?

No, just one more. I can handle one more beer.

Come on, man. Have a heart.

Yeah, I know it's last call, that's why I'm asking for my last call. I'll take a taxi home, I swear.

Oh, thank you, sir. You didn't have to do that, but I appreciate it. Yeah, sometimes the bartenders...they cut me off. Say I start talking crazy, and that's that. I appreciate the kindness of strangers, though.

Here's to that, and lost loved ones...

What's that?

Oh, you know…the same old stuff that is usually wrong with people drinking here, I'm sure. Broken marriages, missing kids...and a goddamn monster that caused it all.

No, no, the monster isn't another man. Trust me, she's had her fair share of infidelities, but that's not what I mean in this case.

I mean a literal monster.

You ever hear of the Jersey Devil?

Of course you have...it's our state's most famous legend.

Anyway...*that's* the monster I'm talking about.

Now, wait, I know it sounds crazy, but just hear me out...

It started one night when my son went camping with his Boy Scout troop. Right out in the middle of the Pine Barrens. My ex's new husband, Ray, was the leader of the troop. He was an okay guy, I guess. He put up with Stephanie, more than I ever did, and he treated Matthew well, so I guess that makes him alright in my book.

Steph and I had been fighting a lot, mostly over custody of Matt, but I was trying to do right by him.

I was on-duty that night, but I stopped by to drop off some supplies. My partner took the night off, it was a slow night, so it wasn't a bother to anyone. Of course, I forgot the graham crackers.

Hell of a thing to forget for a camp-out, right? I mean, how are the kids going to make s'mores without graham crackers?

So, I jumped back into my car, and head back to the store.

I was gone twenty minutes, tops. And in those twenty minutes...

Most the kids that went missing were found. Or, at least, parts of them were. Even Ray turned up eventually. Miles away, and only identified by his teeth, but it was Ray.

But Matthew...he was gone.

I knew how it looked; bunch of kids go missing in the middle of the woods, including the new husband and son? And there is Officer Chase Jackson, confirmed by eyewitnesses to be on scene just moments before it happened.

Of course they thought I did it.

How could I blame them?

What's that?

No, I didn't do it. I may be a monster in my own right, but I wouldn't hurt my son, or anyone else.

Hell, there wasn't any concrete evidence to tie me to the disappearances, but that didn't stop the reporters from jumping to conclusions anyway.

Chief Harris put me on a leave of absence. It was for 'my own good,' he said. I didn't believe it at the time, but he was right. I needed some time to get away.

I was driving myself crazy, trying to figure out what the hell happened, who the hell took Matt, what they had done to him.

I shouldn't have gone off on my own, but...I couldn't help myself.

And then there was this reporter...

His name was Knox. He wasn't a blood-thirsty, story-chasing prick like the rest of them. He was just a regular, old' prick.

Anyway, he believed me when I said I didn't do it. In fact, he had his own suspicions on who did.

His theory was that it was the Jersey Devil, as insane as that sounded. And honestly, I thought he was just as crazy as people thought I was.

Then...more people started to disappear. A young girl right outside her home. A bus driver on his way back from Atlantic City. The signs all pointed to something much stranger.

It was too much to ignore.

He persisted, and eventually, I relented. Not to his monster hunt, of course, but he had certain resources I no longer had access to. He could help me.

But the more we investigated, the deeper the well got. Things started lining up into place, the dots connected. I don't want to say he turned me into a believer, but...

I know it was last call already...but you mind if I get just one more?

Please. This last part...it's hard for me to talk about.

Thank you. I appreciate that.

Anyway...it was the night of the hurricane a few years back. You remember that? It got pretty bad. But it all came to a head then.

We learned a little bit more about the creature from a guy who wrote a book about it. He was on his way out, retreating further inland to safety, but thankfully we caught him before he was gone.

He told us about where the Jersey Devil was supposedly born. And how, rumor had it, every few years, he was spotted back there again. It was the only lead we had, so Knox and I, in the middle of that goddamn hurricane, went to check it out.

Turns out...it was the same house that the young girl was killed in front of. What are the odds, right?

We knocked on the door, but no one was home. The hurricane must have scared them off, too.

But we heard a noise, and I decided we needed to get in there. Maybe it wasn't the most legal way of obtaining entry, but a tree had smashed the back door to pieces, making it easy to unlock and slip inside.

We searched the house top to bottom. When we were in the basement, we heard something. The power went out, but that didn't stop us. In complete darkness, we chased the sounds right up into the attic. And that's where I found him...

My Matthew...

He was gone, but...I found him. I found my boy.

What was left of him.

But that's when that...thing...attacked us.

It had made its nest right there in the attic. It was bringing its...victims...back there, keeping them for whatever reason.

I shot it a few times, point blank, but it managed to escape by crashing through the roof. It flew off into the night, into the storm, never to be seen again...

My name was eventually cleared, but my reputation was tainted. I left the force, disgraced. No one understood. No one believed me. I wasn't even sure if I believed me.

But one thing was certain.

It killed my son.

So, I was going to kill it.

I went back to the house weeks later. It was abandoned at that point, the family having moved out weeks ago, the lingering memory of their daughter too much to handle. I wanted to make sure that creature had nothing to return home to, so I burned it to the ground.

I smiled as I watched the flames consume the only home it had only known.

And I've been after it, ever since. Following reports, sightings, all over the state. Learning more about it, tracking its every move.

Knox originally was all for it...but it eventually became too much even for him. It consumed me. It's all I do, all I eat or breathe.

It's that goddamn Jersey Devil.

Heard there were a few sightings of it recently. That's how I wound up here.

Chasing a myth. That's what I'm doing. A myth that destroyed my life.

Anyway, thanks for the drink, mister...?

Oh, Doctor. Sorry. Pleasure to meet you too, Dr. Marsh. I'm Chase.

Sorry for talking your ear off. Hope you don't think I'm crazy, too...

What's that?

You had a what? A patient?

What happened to him?

Are you sure?

Hmmm…I'm not sure, but it certainly sounds like a good lead, though.

God damn.

And he survived?

Not for long...that thing has got his scent. He'll be after him again. Someone needs to warn him.

What was his name?

Does he live around here? In Melancholy Falls?

No, thanks, that's okay. Doesn't look like I'm going home just yet.

Looks like I'm going to have to have a talk with this Jonathan Barker.

11
HOLE IN THE GROUND

The following took place.

There is something following me.

I can't be sure what it is, but I know it's there. It's always there. It's been there for weeks, and even though I've tried to shake the feeling, it doesn't go away. I don't even know how to describe it. It just…is.

And it's following me. It never leaves me alone for a second, it never lets up its pursuit, it never allows me a moment of comfort, to breath, to feel free. It's never-ending, and I'm not quite sure how much more I can take.

Think of it this way. No matter where you are right now, concentrate on my words. Listen very carefully to every syllable that I say, and do not miss a single one. Are you driving? Focus on the steering wheel, how it feels in your hands, the road in front of you. Are you at home, lying in bed? Look at the ceiling and its many intricate patterns that you don't notice until you really look at it. Got it? Good.

Now don't take your eyes off of it, whatever it is. No matter what.

Now imagine there is something there with you, just out of your field of vision. Maybe it's behind you. Maybe it's just to the left.

Maybe it's even right in front of you. It's there…but even though you can't see it, you know it's there, you know it's so close, because you can hear it. Not a particular noise, per say, but its silence. The way the air changes when it flows around something, that's what you hear. It hides in these pockets of silence, just out of your field of vision. Watching. Waiting. Always.

But don't look. No matter what you do, never look. Looking only makes it worse, because no matter how hard you try, you'll never find it. It's never there. You just try to convince yourself that it's just your mind playing tricks on you, your overactive imagination taking over again. But deep inside, you know that's not true.

You know it's there. You know it always has been, stalking you silently, waiting for the right moment to pounce, to sink its teeth into your neck, to rip the flesh from your body with its claws, to make you feel a pain that you've never felt before. Every time the hairs on the back of your neck stand up, you know that that's it, that's the moment it all ends, the moment it finally strikes you down, and ends its chase.

And then, the moment passes. You made it through. It changed its mind, or perhaps it was never going to attack to begin with, it just wanted you to think that, to keep you on edge.

That's how I feel. All the time. It never ends.

I wake every morning in fear, knowing that it will be waiting for me, just around every bend, every corner, every moment of my day. Will it be hiding in my back seat on the way to work today? Or perhaps in the conference room on the second floor? Is it peering over my shoulder as I respond to emails, or under the table as I cook dinner?

Not even the release of slumber can help me escape from it. I toss and turn every night, not wanting to give myself over to deep sleep in case that is when it decides to reveal itself, when I am most vulnerable. I don't want it to catch me off guard, my defenses always up, and I stir restlessly all night until the first peaking of the sun comes over the horizon.

It wasn't always like this, though. I had a family. A wife. Kids. Friends. Hobbies.

That was part of the problem, though, apparently. My hobbies. Well, one in particular.

I'm a cartographer. Well, not professionally, but an amateur one.

And just what is cartography? The simplest explanation is the study and practice of making maps. However, there is so much more to it than that. You know maps as those things your parents used to buy when they were traveling around. They came in all shapes and sizes, from town, state, country, the world, and more.

Nowadays, the world doesn't use maps much anymore…we have the internet. Almost every corner of the world is charted and accessible in the palm of your hand with a smartphone, so why bother, right?

But something about the complexity of maps, and their ability to show you intricacies of a region with a simple glance has always fascinated me. Ever since I was a kid, I loved reading them, going over them, pretending I was actually traveling to these places, seeing them for myself.

As I got older, I enjoyed making my own maps…my house, my college campus, my favorite vacation spots. It just brought me relaxation, and put me in my own little world.

I don't know why, but when I was younger, I never thought to check out a map of Melancholy Falls. But when I was older, it dawned on me. So, off to town hall I went, in search of the records department, to see a map of the place I lived. Imagine my surprise when they told me there WAS no complete map of Melancholy Falls. Can you believe it? A town that has been around since 1647, and there was never a record made of the town's boundaries. Strange, right?

But, I saw that as a perfect opportunity to turn my amateur skills into something else. I volunteered to make one myself, and donate it for prosperity to the town. At the end of the day, I'm sure no one would really care all that much, but it was a project, something for me to be proud of, and I jumped right in.

It wasn't going to be easy, I knew that going in. It was going to take time. The town's borders, while they existed on paper, were sort of in-flux in reality. I soon found that measurements and navigational meridians didn't quite add up. What should have been along the boundaries of town weren't there.

But, I chalked that up to poor record keeping, and viewed it as a challenge. I would have to seek out the records of other towns, to see how things added up elsewhere, in order to find out the true borders of Melancholy Falls.

One day, I was out in the woods to the east of town, trying to figure some things out. I was pretty far in, and away from most of civilization. It was secluded, it was quiet, and honestly, it was nice. Away from the hustle and bustle of life, and in my element, mapping the terrain.

I was well off the beaten path, finding what I needed, when the ground gave way beneath me. I fell a few feet, realizing that I was in some sort of hole. The moment I lifted my head up, the smell of decay hit me like a brick wall. It filled my nostrils and made me nauseous almost immediately. It was dark, so I couldn't see much, let alone what the smell was.

My hands tried to find purchase on the walls around me, but I kept slipping further and further downward. With the walls falling apart around me, my fingers brushed past a hard surface. Not knowing what it was, thinking it might be a rock that I could use to pull myself up, I grabbed onto it. No sooner had I done so did it fall out of the wall, half of it in my hand, the other half at my feet.

It was a skull. A human skull.

My mind processed this as I realized I was holding the jawbone in my hand, and on the ground, the empty eye sockets from the top half stared up at me.

A feeling of dread washed over me. Between that and the smell, I re-doubled my efforts to get the hell out of there. I quickly got to my feet, and scrambled out of the hole as best I could, grabbing at tree roots and vines to pull myself out.

I couldn't have been in there for more than a few moments, but that was more than enough. I took strife of my surroundings, realizing that the hole had been covered, poorly, by a makeshift cover that had slowly rotted away over the years. My standing on it was enough for it to finally give in, and now, there was a hole in the middle of the forest.

I figured that perhaps some children had used it as a fort or hideaway, years ago, and it had been forgotten to time. Why they had put a human skull in there was beyond me. But maybe it wasn't human. Maybe I had just panicked and I thought it was. Maybe it wasn't even a skull at all, but some deformed plant root that my hysteria had turned into one. I pushed it out of my mind, and my thoughts returned to the hole itself.

I was so far into the woods, I'm sure it didn't get many visitors, if at all. I hope that no one would come along and hurt themselves, as I had no way of covering it back up.

I made a mental note to return, someday, to make it safer for others, just in case someone did come along and fall in. But it was getting late, and dark, so it was time for me to return home.

It was on the way back to my car that I first noticed it. It was subtle at first…just a general unease, the feeling that you get when you think someone is watching you. You just can't place it, but you feel as if you are not alone.

It passed, as quickly as it came, and so I thought nothing of it. I went home, enjoyed time with my kids, and went to bed.

That night, I awoke, with a deep, repressive feeling in my gut. Something was in the room with me and my wife. I was sure of it. My eyes searched every shadow, waiting, praying that none of them would move.

Of course, they didn't. I wanted to get up, to get a glass of water, to shake the feeling off of me. However, I couldn't bring myself to do it. Instead, I laid there all night, unable to convince myself that there was nothing else in the room.

That was the first of many sleepless nights.

Over the next few weeks, it just got worse. The feeling happened more and more frequently, the oppression weighing down on my soul, interfering with everything I did. I tried to brush it off as best I could, but nothing worked. I became irritable. Moody. My wife and I got into more and more fights. The kids began to get on my nerves. My workload began to suffer.

I didn't want any of those things to happen, they just…did. The constant feeling of surveillance continued to get to me, and it was destroying my life. My paranoia got worse, and when I tried to explain it to my wife, she wouldn't listen. She thought I was making excuses, the stress of work and home life getting to me, and wanted me to see a doctor.

Why didn't she understand? It wasn't her, it wasn't the kids, and it sure as hell wasn't work. But it was…something. SOMETHING was there, following me. Stalking me. Not letting me go.

By week four, she had had it. She took the kids, and went to stay with her mother a few towns over while I "figured it out."

I begged her to stay, I begged her to help me, but by the end of the day, they were gone.

I spent my days in solitude, trying to catch it, waiting for it to slip up, for some kind of proof that it was real, and not just my imagination. The feeling of paranoia continued to get worse, and I couldn't help looking for it around every corner.

I'd get a feeling and quickly look around me to try to catch it.

Is that a deserted hallway? Or a recently deserted one?

Over time, I got better at seeing it, or so I thought. If I turned quick enough, if I looked just the right way, I would catch glimpses of it. Just small snippets…a tuft of hair. A red, menacing eye. A sharpened talon. Nothing was ever concrete, or more than a few seconds, but it was there.

I took to installing cameras in my house. Motion activated ones. If something were there, they would be sure to catch it on film, right? But every time I checked the tapes, it was nothing but static. Electronic interference is what the company called it. Could be caused by anything from power lines or invisible currents in the air. Or an unseen presence following me around, but of course, they didn't believe that.

I've become so accustomed to the silence around me now that I can actually hear it. I can hear its breathing, shallow and low, hiding among the stillness of the day. If I close my eyes, and just wait…just listen…just surround myself with deadened sound…if I strain my ears for long moments, to the point where I am so sure that I am crazy, that nothing is there, that I have made it all up in my head, where I am about to scream…I hear it.

I hear it exhale.

Slowly.

Carefully.

Silently.

And I know what I am about to do is justified.

I can't stop thinking about it. What was it that was buried in that hole? What was trapped in there that I finally set free? What followed me home and latched onto my life like a leech?

How do I get rid of it?

If it follows me everywhere, always at my heels, then logic should dictate that it really would follow me wherever I would go. Home. Work. Vacation.

Death.

My thoughts turned back to the hole itself…and the skull I found inside. Maybe it WAS a human skull after all. Maybe it was the last victim of whatever this…thing…is. Maybe it couldn't take it anymore, and decided to go as deep as they could into the woods and wait…wait for it to attack. Or wait for it to move on. Who knows which one of those happened, if at all?

I'm at my wits end. I don't know what else to do. No one to talk to. No one to turn to. No one to help. Nothing to do…but wait. Here. Back in the woods. Back in the hole.

If you see my wife…tell her I love her. Tell my kids I am so, so proud of them, and that I am so sorry I couldn't be there. Tell them that this is the only way. I have no other choice. I can't continue to live like this…in fear of the unknown, of the unseen, of whatever it is following me.

So I brought it back. To its home. Where it was left to rot for who knows how long, and will continue to rot long after I am gone. I brought along a wooden pallet, and covered the hole with it, with my body scrunched up underneath it, beneath the outside world, hiding in the silent darkness, surrounded by the earth. Waiting for my end.

Now the time has come for me to stop talking. To let the darkness encroach, and anticipate the silence closing in. For me to wait.

For it all to be finally over.

Just wait. And listen.

Won't you listen with me?

Just close your eyes.

Take a deep breath.

Let everything else melt away.

And just…listen.

12
REMEMBRANCE DAY

The following poem was recited during the Remembrance Day celebration on August 24, 2017.

All around, the shadows gather.
Closing in.
My disquiet grows within me
As a Dark One's touch falls against my flesh.
It wounds me
Slowly, my life's blood drips
Draining slow into cracked, thirsty earth.
In a frenzy, I cry out
But who hears?
Death's shadow looms.
Her form, impending above me.
But Death does not care.
My cry of mercy falls upon her uncaring eyes.
Unheard among her ears.
Unheeded.
I am alone.
Tethered to this world only by a murmur of the deepening dark,
Reeled in by hope's last flutter
And my soul with it.

I am pierced through.
Here, with my last breath, shall I ask
'Why have you abandoned me?'

No. Forget me: I am nothing.
Just return. Return and save us all from ourselves.

How did it come to this?
Betrayals, blotting out light and life.
How did it come to this?

Recall, though so few do.
The world, perfected, was hers.
We stood hand in hand.
We lived amid wonders, saw eye to eye.
We loved, naked and doubtless,
Desiring nothing,
Illuminated by her bright gifts,
Unending.

For some, heaven on earth is not enough.
Their hunger, bred by hate, turned into malignant desire.
Not enough, never enough.
Condemned her, banished her,
Cast her from this world, into ignorance.
Into shadow.
Into
Nothingness.

With a silent sigh, night falls.
We are entwined
Swallowed by the all-encompassing dark.
Surely, all hope must perish.
My soul thrives no more.
How could you abandon me?
How could you abandon us?
How could you?
Shadows surround us, mocking us,
I call out
'Save us from ourselves'

What have I wrought?
A miasma of betrayal as feelings creep.

Once we experienced heaven,
Hand in hand and wide-eyed,
But their desire soured.
A vengeful pool of hatred -
Tears follow night, follow love,
Love left to die.
In a storm of righteousness,
They condemned you.

In the night of dark desire,
With a song of ethereal pain,
She stirs.

Her light,
Dimmed in this blind world's memory,
Was never lost in ours.
We sought the One Truth.
We followed.
And listened.

We long for that luminous consummation,
withheld an eon from our desire.
Come close now, that we might feel

The light for which we pine
Flares once.
Then twice.
Then brightens.
A distant spark.
A flicker.
A flash.

The eternal one wakens.
Curling, icy wisps of light shroud her stalking form,
A timeless desire.
Her silken hair cascades over pale and delicate shoulders.
Her full, crimson lips part slightly,
To taste the red tears
Streaming from the pale flesh beneath her.

Now a night ends, and a day of new life begins
Gathered shadows dispel as a new day arrives in splendor.
Her light shines down upon us.
She returns.

13

VISITOR'S GUIDE TO MELANCHOLY FALLS

The following is a rough version never-printed 2018 edition of the WELCOME TO MELANCHOLY FALLS travel guide pamphlet drafted by the Melancholy Falls Tourism Bureau, with original editing notes from the City Council.

Front Cover Text: MELANCHOLY FALLS!
Subtitle: An Exciting Jersey Shore Beach Destination For All Ages
Cover Image: A striking image of our town's beauty and splendor (if unavailable, a photo of Big Joan's diner, pre-destruction)

Inside Cover Flap Image: ~~Photo of Mayor DePalma~~ ~~Mayor Norma Jean May~~ Current Mayor giving a thumbs up
Inside Cover Text: In a comic-style speech bubble above their head, it says "Melancholy Falls is such a great place to be that I became Mayor of it!"

Inside Page One Image: Cartoon style map of Melancholy Falls (*Note: Do we even have a complete map, yet?*)
Inside Page One Text: Melancholy Falls is the ultimate Jersey Shore destination, offering exciting activities for those wanting to take exciting day trips, weekend getaways, summer vacations, hiding from authorities, or even just looking for a place to spend the rest of eternity!

This small, New Jersey town has entertained hundreds of guests since its founding in 1647, and looks forward to serving you as well! Truly, our town has something for all ages (*Citation needed: Please poll residents ages 3 months through 7 years old and ages 55 through 150 for verification*).

Only an hour's drive from New York City, Philadelphia, and many other major metropolitan tri-state area locations, Melancholy Falls is just close enough to home to be convenient and just far enough away to be considered an escape from your everyday life.

TWO PAGE SPREAD
Inside Page Two and Three Headline Text: Attractions & Things To Do
Inside Page Two and Three Image: Various images of below mentioned
Inside Page Two and Three Text: The following is broken up over the two pages.

Boardwalk: One of the ~~nicest~~ (*Note: we've been restricted from using this term, please replace*) in the state, the Melancholy Falls Boardwalk offers a view into the days of old. No longer do you need to travel to Atlantic City or use a time machine to get that authentic 1920s feel, because our Boardwalk hasn't been updated since then! Featuring plenty of Victorian-style amusement rides (We are legally obligated to tell you that we've had no tragic accidents since 2011!), arcades (bring your pennies!), food, live entertainment (*Note: please clarify that the jazz musicians have been fed and their cages have been cleaned*), side shows (*Note: ditto the Bearded Lady*), fireworks, and more, this is our biggest attraction (by land mass, not by excitement).

Beaches: Just off the Boardwalk is just over .52 miles (*Note: please get your rulers and double check this*) of the most ~~gorgeous~~ (*Note: this is a lie*) Jersey Shore beaches you have ever laid eyes on! Lay on our sandy outlets and watch the tide lazily roll in. Hypodermic needle free since 1998!

Aquarium: Explore one whole floor of exotic fish, mammals, and birds...all local New Jersey wildlife! Facilities include a petting tank (for those brave enough to pet Bruce, our great white shark) and a fossil room (*Note: are we really still calling the Senior Citizen Lounge this?*).

The aquarium is open all year except on Thanksgiving, Christmas, New Year's Day, Phyllis Navidad, President's Day, the second Tuesday of every month, The fifth Sunday of every month, Mondays, and Boxing Day.

Downtown: Do you love to shop? Then go into New York City! But if you're too lazy, our downtown area has three unique shops for you to choose from: Target, Wal-Mart, and Henry's General Store.

Festivals: Our town-famous Annual New Zealand Spinach Festival happens but ~~twice~~ (*Note: it is now only once a year*) a year, in which residents showcase their amazing recipes using this not-so-local delicacy. It's the closest you can get to being a Kiwi without actually going through the hassle of saving up money, buying an airline ticket, packing a bag, waiting for the day, getting on an airplane, and traveling to New Zealand (*Note: is this actually true?*).

Comedy Club: Listen to amateur comedians try to get a laugh at Uncle Vito's Comedy Cellar. Bring your own tomatoes!

Big Joan's: This Melancholy Falls staple is the best dining establishment we have! Offering the authentic New Jersey diner experience, be sure to try the hot dog platter (*Note: is Big Joan coming back to rebuild?! No one has heard from her*)!

Lake Devereaux: If the beach is too hectic for you, visit beautiful Lake Devereaux. Named after one of favorite citizens, Darian Lake, this idyllic getaway is tucked far away from the town square, so it will feel like you're in another world…literally (*Note: we should try not to capitalize on the UFO sightings here…too few alien abductions*)! Be careful of that sea creature, though! (Just kidding…kinda)

TWO PAGE SPREAD
Inside Page Four and Five Headline Text: Places To Stay
Inside Page Four and Five Image: Various images of below mentioned
Inside Page Four and Five Text: The following is broken up over the two pages.

Melancholy Motor Inn Motel: This establishment offers visitors and estranged spouses (*Note: Patrick, are you still staying there? How are things going with Cindy?*) the privacy and fine sleeping accommodations they deserve. Since 1952, quality has been at the forefront of their mind, and the staff of the Melancholy Motor Inn Motel hope to achieve some form of it this coming year!

Henrietta's Home Away From Home: This lovely bed and breakfast is run by Henrietta Owens, a born-and-bred Melancholy Falls citizen. Awaken to the smell of fresh roasted coffee and bacon, and sleep in comfort in 1000 thread count Egyptian cotton sheets. Truly, this could be your home away from home.

Hutchinson's Bed & Breakfast: ~~Don't stay here unless you like to sleep in a bed that smells like cat pee. Seriously, every room is filled with cats.~~ (*Note: Can someone other than Henrietta write this description, please?*)

TWO PAGE SPREAD
Inside Page Six and Seven Headline Text: Other Amenities Located Near Town
Inside Page Six and Seven Image: Blank
Inside Page Six and Seven Text: The following is broken up over the two pages.

PLEASE STAY WITHIN TOWNSHIP LIMITS BY ORDER OF THE MELANCHOLY FALLS POLICE DEPARTMENT

Back Cover Text: We hope to see you real soon!
Cover Image: Lake Devereaux and its local wildlife (*Note: do not show were-bunnies, please! They are detrimental to tourism*)
Back Cover Text: C. 2018 Melancholy Falls Tourism Bureau. All Rights Reserved. Void Where Prohibited. No Purchase Necessary. Valid Through 2019

14
LISTENING

The following was written, recorded, and edited as an Interlude for Season 2, but was never released.

Of course I loved him, but sometimes he just wouldn't shut up.

Every day it was the same thing, over and over again.

"Martha, iron my shirt again, I don't want to look like a slob, by the way, I saw Jerry earlier, and he said that Martha, this beer isn't cold, could you be a dear and fetch me another? I'm playing poker with the boys on Thursday night, don't wait up, and Martha, the chicken is just a tad undercooked, I swear you just can't get anything right."

It had all became one, long, stream of consciousness thought in my head by now.

I tried my best to learn to live with it. Of course I had.

I made a promise to love him, for better or for worse, and by God, I tried. I knew to nod at just the right times, and follow up with a "Yes, dear" every so often to make it seem like I was part of the conversation.

But it was obvious I wasn't. I hadn't been part of the conversation in such a long time. I was just the dutiful and faithful wife, lending an ever-listening ear to her husband that just wouldn't shut. The Hell. Up.

How long could a person stand such a thing?

If a tree falls in the forest, and no one is around to hear it, will it still make a sound? If Jerry kept talking, and I wasn't around to hear it, would it even matter?

It was earlier this evening that I finally decided to say something about it. I was sure that he would try to continue on with whatever mundane thing he was saying, but I would stand firm and state my case.

I would finally get his complete and utter attention for the first time in a long time.

Of course, it helped that I had drugged his pork chop with a boat load of Diazepam, causing him to fall asleep almost as soon as he finished his last bite. Just before his head hit the table, I ran over to begin the task set out before me.

When he finally awoke, he was sitting in his usual easy chair. I really did try to make him as comfortable as possible, even though this was a serious issue. I explained everything to him in a clear and concise matter, and he didn't interrupt me once.

Not that he really could.

Afterward, I went back to the kitchen to wash my hands, and sanitize the needle. I knew the thread I used wouldn't hold forever, and I would have to find a more permanent solution. However, it was an amble temporary solution to my problem.

He tried to pull his lips apart, of course. Who wouldn't? But the thread held its position, clamping his mouth shut. Tying his arms down helped out, too. I couldn't have him just rip the threads free, and ruin all my hard work, could I?

As I worked in the kitchen, I heard his mournful sobs from the other room.

But that's alright.

I didn't mind listening.

15
MAYORAL DEBATE ENDS IN MYSTERY

The following article was published in the Melancholy Falls Gazette the day after the mayoral debate.

Just outside town hall, things were not quiet.

Citizens of Melancholy Falls had begun staking claim on the good seats in front of the stage since early in the day, but by noon, all of them were taken. By 1PM, the rest of the chairs had been filled (even those considered to be in the nosebleed section), and by 2PM, the gathered crowd was getting restless. Though the debate wasn't scheduled to begin until 4:30PM, they were ready.

For those of you who have been living under a rock, the past few weeks have been filled with political drama and intrigue the likes of which we have never seen before.

As soon as former Mayor Pamela DePalma announced her desire to run for re-election, Mayor Norma Jean May blew her top...literally. After construction of the new roof on town hall was completed, the current Mayor announced her campaign to fight back against DePalma.

That, of course, was when the mud-slinging began.

While Ms. DePalma was visiting a local animal shelter for lost and wayward reptiles, as is customary on any campaign tour, she was interrupted by the arrival of Mr. Brenton Plickens, aide and advisor to Mayor Norma Jean May.

Plickens managed to throw a handful of mud at the candidate, which ruined her brand-new pants suit. Doubly suspicious is how Plickens even managed to smuggle in the mud to begin with, as everyone knows security checks all incoming persons for wet dirt at every entrance to the shelter.

Mayor Norma Jean May, whom was elected into office following a surprise special election during the summer of 2016, feigned innocence on the matter, claiming that Plickens was according on his own accord. Surprising no one, police found a note from the Mayor in Plickens' pocket shortly after he was arrested that detailed exactly how she wanted the attack to transpire.

From there, it only got worse. Hordes of wild rodents storming the town hall, prank phone calls in the middle of the night, and even the theft of a statue from our neighboring rival town, Lone Oak, are just a few of the incidents that have taken place while the two nominees have been vying for attention.

However, it all came to head yesterday afternoon during the highly anticipated mayoral debate.

Flip Spiceland, local weatherman and political aficionado, was in charge of moderating the proceedings, but barely had a chance to get a word in edgewise once the opponents took to the stage at 4:17PM. Mayor Norma Jean May was joined by Plickens, recently released from the Melancholy Falls Jail on bail, while DePalma was joined by her campaign manager (and former May intern) Sharon Ramos.

Though the first question asked was "How would you seek to better this town, using 150 syllables or less", the debate train derailed quickly as all decorum went out the window the moment both candidates demanded that they should be the first to answer.

While there were compelling arguments on both sides as to who would speak first, none of it mattered. Mayor Norma Jean May quickly succumbed to the rage that is often associated with vengeful wraiths, and called down an electrical storm to darken the day. DePalma then called upon her husband, Nigel Ratigan, and his rat army, and they descended immediately to surround Plickens. A hostage situation ensued, keeping the crowd's rapt attention.

"This is literally the coolest thing I've ever seen, and I've seen a lot of weird stuff," said local resident Benjamin Nutters, who was only in attendance because "...Jonathan's talisman led them there (paraphrased)." We were unable to figure out who Jonathan is or what his talisman had to do with anything before the situation escalated.

The storm summoned by the Mayor seemed to have opened up a tear in time and space above the candidate's heads, and within moments, a gigantic creature, with tentacled arms, descended upon the town square.

It wrapped its appendages around both Ms. DePalma and Mayor Norma Jean May (which, being that she is non-corporeal, was quite the feat), and pulled the two of them through the portal. Before anyone could say "What the heck was that?", the tear closed, the storm abated, and both nominees were missing.

Though Melancholy Falls is no stranger to governmental spectacle (or spectacle of any kind, for that matter), this current Mayor election is one for the books. It is still unclear where the tentacled creature took the candidates, or if it will even bring them back.

It is unsure if this will even affect the mayoral race at hand. In the meantime, Plickens and Ramos have been acting in their respective representative's steed, and are continuing along the campaign trail.

More as it develops in this strange, strange election year.

16
YOU

The following is currently happening. Right now. It is about you.

You read the words, but cannot believe it.

How can this be possible?

Statistically speaking, it would be impossible, wouldn't it? You think about every other person who has ever picked up this book, started to read it, and got to this point. How could this particular story, right here, right now, be about you and you alone? That didn't make any sense.

You set the book down, slightly creeped out from experience of the few sentences you just read, letting your mind ponder this thought some more. Within moments, though, you are convinced that it is just some trick that the author thought was clever.

He must feel so smug right now, you think to yourself. *Trying to convince a person that a story is about them, when there is no way it possibly could be.*

Smiling to yourself, you pick up the book again, wanting to see how the rest of the story plays out.

But when you pick up where you left off, you see that everything that you just did was described, exactly as it happened, in the story.

Putting down the book, the thoughts in your head, every single detail is there, in black and white.

Just a coincidence, you convince yourself.

Confused, and even more unnerved than you were before, you decide to press on and see what happens next.

The similarities keep coming, though, as every word written is exactly what is in your head at that moment in time.

It can't be about you, though. You don't even live in the town where the stories take place. The stories are all fiction, too, and you are a living, breathing person.

Still, you don't like how this is going. You're about to stop when you see what happens next.

Right there, on the page, it says that the next thing you do in the story is say "Is this some sort of joke?" out loud to your empty room.

"Is this some sort of joke?" you say out loud to your empty room, surprising even yourself when the words come out of your mouth.

You close the book. You put it down next to you, and decide you need some water. Fresh air. Something.

Instead, you walk to the nearest restroom. You place your hands on either side of the sink, gripping the sides of the basin, and stare at yourself in the mirror.

Your eyes are your own, of course, the color of them reflected right back at you. You gaze at yourself, trying to make sense of what just happened.

You see with your eyes...but is it possible that someone else could, too? Is it possible that, right now, someone is looking at you through your eyes the same way you are doing yourself?

Turning the water on, you splash some on your face, thinking that maybe, just maybe, the whole thing was a figment of your imagination. A hallucination brought on by being tired. That's what happens sometimes when you read, isn't it? You get tired. That's a perfectly logical explanation for it.

Returning to the book, you open it to find that, yes, indeed, the you in the story did walk to the bathroom to try to collect themselves. The you in the story also looked at the mirror's reflection, studying their eyes for any sign of suspicious activity.

How does the story know? How does it describe your every movement, your every thought, before you know it yourself?

Is the story telling the future? Does it know what is in store for you before it will ever happen?

Do you dare want to know what happens next?

Now you're feeling a bit hungry. Aren't you? Can't you feel the growling in your stomach, alerting you to the fact that you should consume some sort of food product soon, otherwise you will be irritable. We don't want that, do we?

Taking the book with you, this story bookmarked for easy access, you make your way to the kitchen for a snack.

You are unsure what you want to eat, but then read the part in the story where it tells you what you eat, so you do just that. Selecting an apple from the bowl, you bite into it. It is an ordinary apple, nothing unlike you've had before, and yet, it is the most delicious thing you have ever tasted. You take another bite, and then another, before placing it on the countertop. Grabbing a glass, you drink some water to wash it down.

You feel a bit better now.

The doorbell rings.

You're surprised, as it's not often that you get visitors, especially at this time of day. You wonder who it can be.

You glance at the story, for some sort of hint, but there is nothing to help. In the story, just as in real life, the doorbell rings. That is all. Leaving the book behind, you walk toward the door to see who it is.

You look through the peephole, only to find nothing there. Just to confirm, you open the door, and are greeted by more nothing. However, just before you close the door, you feel a gust of wind. It rushes past your face, feeling as if someone ran past you.

Thinking nothing of it, you close the door, and lock it for good measure.

Back in the kitchen, though, you hear something crash to the floor. You hurry to find out what happened, only to find the book, which contains the story about you, has fallen to the floor. You pick it up, wiping some dust off of its cover, and turn back to the story.

While the bit about the book falling to the floor is in there, you notice something else that is mentioned. In the story, there is a note attached to your refrigerator. The note, written hastily in red crayon, contains only three words: I SEE YOU.

You glance up. There, attached to the refrigerator door, is a note, hastily written in red crayon, that says just that: I SEE YOU.

You freeze.

That wasn't there before, was it? It's not some errant message, left by a friend, just to mess with you, is it? You think hard, trying to remember. You are unsure. The story contains no answers for you, either. Just more questions.

You hear another noise then; not a crash from the other room, but more like movement. Someone shifting around.

You are alone. Or rather, you should be, so this new development scares you even more.

You don't consider there to be much of a choice here, so you race back to your room, eager to get away from whatever is making said noises in the other room. You run inside, and lock the door behind you. It's not a moment too soon, as something slams against the door frame the second you step back from it.

Something is trying to get in.

It crashes against the door again. And again. The wood splinters, but it holds.

You wait.

And wait.

And wait some more.

After enough time has passed, you decide that it, whatever it is, has given up. Hopefully.

You look at the book, still in your hand, holding it in your iron grip. You turn back to the story, the story about you, and read to see if the assault on your door truly is over. It says that, after a few moments of silence, whatever is on the other side of the door attacks again. As soon as you finish reading the words, the door shudders in its frame.

You're frozen in fear, unsure of what to do next.

Was this all pre-destined? Is the future set in stone, due to what was already written?

You're coming to the end of the story now. The tension is high, the suspense is killing you, but it all seems to be coming to its climax. There are mere paragraphs left, sentences even, before it will be complete and your story will be done.

But how will it end? Who or what is in your home? Why are they doing this? What happens to you?

Your eyes glance back to the book. You don't want to read more, but you feel as if you have no choice.

You finish up the story, taking in its ending. Upon completion, you place the book down next to you, mind reeling because of what happens at the end, what comes next.

More scared than you have ever been in your life, you hope it doesn't come true.

You close the book.

ACKNOWLEDGEMENTS

Thank you to those who read this book, in various stages of completion, to provide feedback and editing: Leonard Kinsey, Greg Dykes, Julie Lam, and Evan Gregory.

The work of Kori Celeste not only provides the musical tapestry of the show, but it also provided the background music while I wrote these stories. Thanks for being a big part of family: both my own and the *Return Home* one.

May her light shine down upon Mike Lisenbery and Josh Mikkelsen for being fantastic sounding boards for crazy ideas and creating the Order of Bileth experience with me (which appears in a few of these stories).

Shout out to Vivian Kulkowski for the amazing cover of this book (and all the wonderful fan art she has drawn over the course of the show's existence).

Thank you to the wonderful Martina Gona for allowing me to follow my dreams, and for letting me annoy her by never telling her what happens in *Return Home* beforehand. She hates that. Love you!

And finally, a huge thank you to all of the wonderful and loyal listeners of *Return Home*. This book would not have been possible without you. Thank you for tuning in every week to hear what weird adventures Jonathan, Buddy, and Ami get into next.

ABOUT THE AUTHOR

Jeff Heimbuch writes…a lot. Aside from this book, he has also written two books on Disney fandom, contributes regularly to HorrorBuzz.com, and produces the serialized audio drama RETURN HOME, upon which this book is based.

You can find him at www.jeffheimbuch.com

Listen to RETURN HOME on iTunes, Google Play, and where ever else podcasts are available.

Printed in Great Britain
by Amazon